For Will and his doggie,
Nate and his bunny,
Sylvie and her teddy,
Charlie and his puppy,
and Lucy and her pink mimi.

— H.M.Z.

Text copyright © 2011 by Harriet Ziefert
Illustrations copyright © 2011 by Barroux
All rights reserved / CIP Data is available.
Published in the United States 2011 by
🍎 Blue Apple Books, 515 Valley Street, Maplewood, NJ 07040
www.blueapplebooks.com
First Edition   03/11 Printed in Dongguan, China
ISBN: 978-1-60905-028-3

2 4 6 8 10 9 7 5 3 1

Harriet Ziefert

Bunny's Lessons

paintings by **BARROUX**

Blue Apple Books

He's Charlie.
I'm his bunny.

Charlie is my friend.
My teacher.
Whatever I know,
I learned from Charlie.

Charlie likes to make music.
When he practices the tuba,

I learn about **LOUD.**

When we play doctor,
Charlie is the boss.

I learn about

OUCH!

Charlie likes buttered noodles for lunch.

I learn about

MESSY.

When Charlie is the dad,
I am the baby.

I learn about

Pretend.

Sometimes Charlie interrupts.

When Charlie is
RUDE...

Go to your room.

I learn about **TIME-OUT.**

Today, Charlie has a playdate.

Charlie and his girlfriend
play with other toys
and he forgets about me.

I learn about

JEALOUS.

Charlie's favorite word is

MORE.

All I hear is . . .

and **MORE!**

More is fun
most of the time,
but not always.

More is not fun when Charlie paints.
He paints everything—
including **ME!**

I don't like being covered in paint.
Charlie apologizes and says,

"Sorry."

But I'm still dirty.
And blue.

Then Charlie gives me a bath.

I learn how **sorry**

can become

all better!

If Charlie is

SCARED...

I stay close.

But Charlie does not always stay with me.

Now I am **ALONE.**

I am
lonely.

And
SCARED.

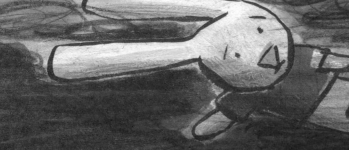

And SAD.

When Charlie finds me and gives me a hug,

I learn about **LOVE.**

The end